Waltz

For ANNE *and* ANDREA

THE SLEEPING BEAUTY

The Sleeping

From *the Tales of* CHARLES PERRAULT

Music by PETER ILYICH TSCHAIKOVSKY

Beauty

Adapted and Illustrated by

WARREN CHAPPELL

Schocken Books • *New York*

First published by Schocken Books 1982
10 9 8 7 6 5 4 3 2 1   82 83 84 85
Published by arrangement with Alfred A. Knopf, Inc.

Library of Congress Cataloging in Publication Data
Chappell, Warren, 1904– The sleeping beauty. Adaptation of: La belle au bois dormant /
Charles Perrault. Reprint. Originally published: New York : Knopf, 1961. Summary:
Enraged at not being invited to the princess' christening, the wicked fairy casts a spell that
dooms the princess to sleep for 100 years. Includes examples of themes from the score of
Tschaikovsky's ballet.
[1. Fairy tales.   2. Folklore—France]   I. Tschaikovsky, Peter Ilich, 1840–1893.   II. Per-
rault, Charles, 1628–1703. Belle au bois dormant. English.   III. Sleeping beauty. English.
IV. Title.
[PZ8.C3665S   1981]   398.2'1'0944   81–40405   AACR2

Music adapted from the score of *The Sleeping Beauty*
by permission of the Tschaikovsky Foundation

Manufactured in the United States of America
ISBN 0–8052–0683–3

Entrance
of the
Guests

THE PROMISES

THERE were once a King and a Queen who had no children, and this grieved them more than words can tell. They went to all the healing waters in the world. They made vows and did everything they could think of, but to no avail.

At last, however, the Queen did have a baby—a little girl. There was a fine christening party, and all the fairies in the kingdom—there were seven of them—were made godmothers to the Princess. This was done in order that each of the fairies might give the Princess a gift, as was the custom at that time, and so endow her with all the good qualities imaginable. After the christening, the guests came back to the King's palace, where a great banquet was

The
Good Fairies

held in honour of the fairies. They sat at a table where a rich cloth
was spread for them, and on the cloth were seven golden caskets,
one for each of the fairies. Every casket contained a knife, a fork,
and a spoon, all of fine gold and studded with rubies and diamonds.

Just as the guests sat down, in came an old fairy who had not
been invited because for more than fifty years she had not come out
of her tower. She was thought to be dead, or perhaps under a spell.
The King had a place laid for her, but he could not give her a gold-
en casket because only the set of seven had been made. The old
fairy thought she was being slighted, and she grumbled to herself
in a threatening way. One of the younger fairies sitting beside her
heard this, and feared the angry old creature might give the little
Princess some unlucky gift. She hid behind the curtains when the
banquet was over, in order to be the last one to speak. In this way,
she hoped to put right, as far as she was able, any harm the old
fairy might do.

Now the fairies began to present their gifts. The youngest promised that the Princess should be the most beautiful girl in all the world; the next, that she should be the wittiest; the third, that whatever she did, she should do most gracefully; the fourth, that she should dance perfectly; the fifth, that she should sing like a nightingale; and the sixth, that she should be able to play sweetly on all kinds of musical instruments.

It was now the old fairy's turn. Wagging her head more in spite than from old age, she foretold that the Princess would prick herself with a distaff, and that would be the death of her. Everyone shuddered at such a terrible curse, and they all burst into tears. But at that moment the young fairy stepped from behind the curtains and said in a loud voice: "Take courage, Your Majesties; your daughter will not die. I cannot undo completely what my older sister has prophesied, and the Princess will indeed prick her finger with a distaff. But instead of dying, she will only fall into a deep

The
Evil Fairy

Andantino

sleep which shall last a hundred years. At the end of that time, a
King's son shall come and wake her!"

The King tried to avert the ill fortune foretold by the old fairy.
He proclaimed that no one should be allowed to spin with a distaff,
or even have a distaff in the house, on pain of death.

*The
Evil Fairy's
Prediction*

THE SLEEP

FIFTEEN or sixteen years went by. The King and Queen were away at one of their country houses, and the little Princess, having nothing else to do, went roaming about the palace. She wandered from room to room, and from floor to floor, until she came to the top of one of the towers. There she found a tiny attic, where a kindly old woman was sitting and spinning. This old woman had never heard of the King's orders against using the distaff.

"What are you doing, good woman?" asked the Princess.

"Why, I'm spinning, my pretty dear," answered the woman, who did not know who her visitor was.

"It looks very interesting," said the Princess. "May I try to spin?"

No sooner had she taken hold of the distaff than she pricked her finger, partly because she was rather hasty and snatched, but mostly because the wicked fairy would have it so. She fell down in a faint, and when the kindly old woman shouted for help, people came running from all over the palace. They dashed water over the Princess, they loosened her bodice, they patted her hands and rubbed her temples with a sweet-smelling scent, but nothing would revive her.

Meanwhile, the King had returned. Hearing so much commotion, he rushed up to the tower, and when he saw his daughter he remembered the fairy's curse. Knowing that what had been foretold would have to be, he had the Princess carried to the best room in the palace, where she was laid on a bed all hung with silver and gold brocade. She was so beautiful that she looked like an angel. The bright colour of her complexion had not faded at all, and her

cheeks were like pale pink carnations, her lips like coral. Only her eyes were closed. The King could hear her breathing softly, and he knew his lovely daughter could not be dead. He ordered his people to leave her in peace, until the hour should come for her to awaken.

When the accident occurred, the good fairy who had saved the life of the Princess was in a distant kingdom, twelve thousand leagues away. But she was told what had happened within an instant, by a dwarf wearing magic boots in which he could cover many miles at a single stride. The good fairy set out at once and arrived at the King's palace in an hour, driving a chariot drawn by dragons all of fire.

The King came out and gave her his arm as she dismounted. She said he had done all for the best. But as she always thought of everything beforehand, she knew that the Princess would be very lonely in that great palace when she at last awoke. So this is what she did. She touched everyone in the palace with her magic wand, except the King and Queen. She touched the governesses, the maids of honour, the waiting gentlewomen, the gentlemen of the bedchamber, the officers, the stewards, the cooks, the scullions, the grooms, the guards, the ushers, the pages, the footmen. She touched

all the horses in the stables, and the stable boys too, the mastiffs in the yard, and Pouffle, the Princess's little lapdog, who was curled up on her bed. As soon as the good fairy touched them, they all fell asleep, not to wake up until their mistress needed them again. Even the spit in front of the kitchen fire, on which partridges and pheasants were roasting, stopped turning, and the fire died down. It was all done in a moment.

Then the King and Queen, having kissed their dear child, left the palace. In no time at all, there grew up along the borders of the grounds such a quantity of trees both great and small, of briars and brambles all twined together, that neither man nor beast could get through it. Nothing could be seen, even from a great way off, but the tops of the palace towers. The fairy had done this on purpose, so that the Princess would not be bothered by anyone during her long sleep.

Andante misterioso

The
Sleep

THE AWAKENING

A HUNDRED years went by. Another royal family had come to the throne in that kingdom. One day, the son of the reigning King was out hunting, near the old palace. He could see the tops of the towers above the trees, and he asked about them in a nearby village. Some of the villagers said a haunted castle was in the middle of that great wood, others said it was the place where witches held their meetings. The most common opinion was that a great ogre lived there, and that he was never followed because he alone was able to force his way through the wood.

The Prince did not know what to believe. Then an old, old countryman spoke up and said: "Your Highness, it's more than

The Prince

Sees a Vision

of the

Princess

fifty years since I heard my father say that there was a Princess in that castle, the prettiest one that ever was seen. And she was bound to sleep there a hundred years, and be awakened by a King's son, who would be the one for her."

When he heard this, the young Prince felt himself all on fire. He resolved to put the story to a test then and there. He advanced on the wood, and as he did so, all the briars and brambles and all the great trees bent back to let him pass. He went toward the palace along a great avenue of trees, and was surprised to see that none of his servants could follow because the trees had closed up behind him as soon as he had passed by.

The Prince came into a great forecourt. There was a frightful silence everywhere. Bodies of men and of animals were stretched all about. But at a second glance, the Prince could see that the ushers' noses were red and their cheeks were ruddy, and he knew they were only asleep. The goblets in their hands still held a few

drops of wine, to show that they had fallen asleep while drinking.

From a large courtyard paved in marble, the Prince ascended a staircase and entered a guard-room, where the guards were drawn up with their muskets on their shoulders, all snoring away. He passed through room after room full of ladies and gentlemen in waiting, all fast asleep, some of them sitting and some on their feet.

At last he came to a room with golden panelling, and there on a bed with all its curtains drawn back was the most beautiful sight he had ever beheld. A Princess, who seemed to be about fifteen or sixteen years old, was lying on the bed; she looked radiantly beautiful. Trembling all over, the Prince came nearer to admire her, and fell to his knees beside her. At that moment the spell was broken. The Princess awoke. She looked at the Prince tenderly indeed, considering it was the first time she had set eyes on him, and she said: "Is it you, my Prince? You have been a long time coming."

The Prince was overjoyed to hear the Princess speak these

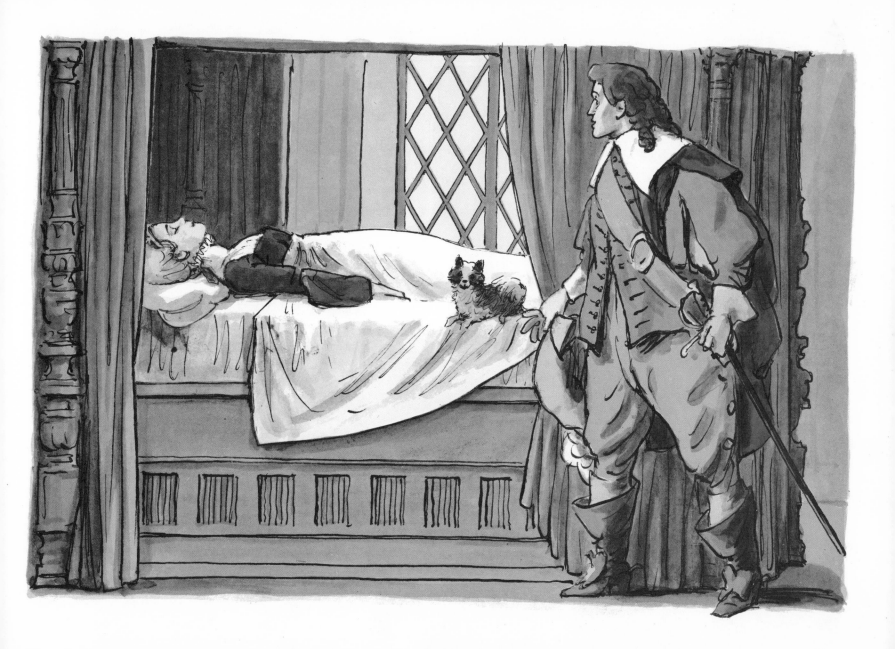

words. He assured her that he loved her better than life itself. The other things he told her were rather confusing; they both cried a good deal, and were tongue-tied with love. He was in even greater confusion than she was, and no wonder, for she had had time to think over what she would say. The good fairy, it seems, had arranged for her to have pleasant dreams during her long sleep. The Prince and Princess talked for four hours without getting to the end of half the things they meant to tell each other.

Meanwhile, all the palace had come to life when the Princess awakened. The fire in the kitchen burst into flame, the spits with partridges and pheasants on them began to turn. Pouffle, the Princess's lap dog, opened his eyes, the mastiffs in the courtyard stretched themselves. Stable boys and their horses, footmen, pages, ushers, guards, grooms, scullions, cooks, and stewards took up their duties again. The officers of the palace, ladies and gentlemen in

The
Princess's
Dance

waiting, maids of honour and governesses went about their business as if nothing had happened.

But they were not all in love, and they felt ravenously hungry. One of the maids of honour, losing her patience, called out to her mistress that dinner was ready. The Prince helped the Princess rise from the bed on which she had slept for a hundred years. She was dressed in magnificent clothes, but the Prince had the good sense not to tell her that what she was wearing was the style in his great-grandmother's time. She was none the less beautiful for that.

They went into the great dining-hall, where dinner was served by members of the Princess's household. A band of violins and oboes played quaint old music most sweetly—tunes that had not been heard for many years. And so it came to pass that after much joyful feasting, the Princess and her Prince were married in the palace chapel, and they lived happily ever after.

CHARLES PERRAULT   (*1628–1703*)

French poet and critic who published his *Contes du temps passé ou contes de ma mere L'oie* in 1697. These stories included such classics as *Little Red Riding-Hood*, *Bluebeard*, *Puss-in-Boots*, *Tom Thumb*, *Cinderella*, and *The Sleeping Beauty*.

PETER ILYICH TSCHAIKOVSKY   (*1840–93*)

Russian pianist, composer and conductor, pupil of Rubenstein. In addition to writing the score for *The Sleeping Beauty* ballet, he composed the music for *The Nutcracker*.

Waltz